Edgar Badger's Balloon Day

Edgar Badger's Balloon Day

by Monica Kulling

illustrated by
Carol O'Malia

MONDO

For my parents, Anita and Walter, with love — M.K.

With loving thanks to my parents,
Mildred and Charles O'Malia — C.O'M

Text copyright © 1996 by Monica Kulling
Illustrations copyright © 1996 by Carol O'Malia

For information contact:
MONDO Publishing
One Plaza Road
Greenvale, New York 11548

Visit our web site at http://www.mondopub.com

Story previously published in *Ladybug*, the Magazine for Young Children,
as "Duncan Bear's Balloon Day."

Designed by Eliza Green
Production by The Kids at Our House

Printed in Hong Kong by South China Printing Co. (1988) Ltd.
97 98 99 00 01 02 03 04   9 8 7 6 5 4 3 2

Library of Congress Cataloging-in-Publication Data
Kulling, Monica.
    Edgar Badger's balloon day / by Monica Kulling ; illustrated by Carol
O'Malia.
        p.   cm.
    Summary: Edgar Badger is convinced that his friends have forgotten
his birthday.
        ISBN 1-57255-220-4 (pbk. : alk. paper)
        [1. Badgers—Fiction. 2. Birthdays—Fiction. 3. Animals—Fiction.]
I. O'Malia, Carol, ill. II. Title.
PZ7.K940155E 1996
[E]—dc20   96-15259
                                                                CIP
                                                                 AC

Contents

A Knock at the Door • 7

Busy Friends • 17

The Wrong Day? • 29

Surprise! • 39

A Knock at the Door

Edgar Badger hopped out of bed. He did a jig around his room.

"Today's my balloon day," he sang.

"Today's my Happy Birthday balloon day!"

Edgar Badger loved balloons.
Balloons made him feel happy.
Balloons made him feel light.

Edgar was a big badger. He didn't
often feel light. Balloons made him
feel like he could float on air.

Suddenly there was a knock at the door.

"My first Happy Birthday," sang Edgar as he waddled to the door. "Maybe even my first birthday present!"

Duncan Bear was at the door.

"Good morning Edgar," said Duncan.

"Time you were out and about."

"It *is* a good morning," agreed Edgar.
He smiled his best birthday smile and
waited.

But Duncan didn't hold out a present. Duncan held out a cup.

"What's this?" Edgar asked.

"Flour," replied Duncan. "I need a cup of flour."

"A cup of flour?" asked Edgar. "Is that all?"

"Yes, that's all," Duncan answered.

"Are you sure?" Edgar wanted to know.

"Sure, I'm sure," said Duncan. "I'm out of flour. No doubt about it."

"You came all the way over here just for flour?" Edgar asked.

"Not another thing," replied Duncan. "Just flour."

Edgar sighed. *Duncan has such a poor memory,* he thought. *He's forgotten my birthday.*

Edgar gave Duncan the flour. Then he went back inside to make breakfast.

"Duncan doesn't know it's my birthday," said Edgar sadly. "Maybe no one does."

Suddenly Edgar's stomach did a flip-flop. He put down his spoon. He couldn't eat one more bite of his hickory-nut cereal.

"I have to do something," he said. "I can't let my birthday go by without at least one balloon!"

Edgar left his breakfast. He ran
out of his house.

Busy Friends

*E*dgar tromped along in the woods.
Birds sang in the trees. Butterflies
danced through the leaves. It was
a marvelous day for a birthday.

Amanda Salamander was sitting on a rock. She was tying knots with a ball of string. She was making a net.

"Beautiful day, isn't it?" said Edgar.

"Beautiful," agreed Amanda. She kept on knotting.

"It's a special day, too," said Edgar.

Amanda stopped knotting.

"Special?" she asked. "Why is today special?"

"Today is special," said Edgar,
"because today is . . . today is . . ."

Edgar wanted to say it was his
birthday. But he couldn't. Friends
should remember your birthday,
shouldn't they?

"I guess it's only special to me,"
said Edgar. He sighed and slowly
walked away.

Sally Otter was down by the river.
She was making a strange boat,
but Edgar didn't notice. He had
only one thing on his mind.

"When do you think is the best time
for a birthday?" Edgar asked Sally.

Sally was busy hammering. Nails
stuck out of her mouth. She didn't
even look up.

"I think summer is best," said Edgar.
"If I had a winter birthday I would
change it. But I'm lucky. I don't have
to do that."
Sally wasn't listening. She was
too busy hammering.

Edgar sighed and slowly walked away. What an awful day. What a terrible day. What an awful, terrible birthday!

The Wrong Day?

*H*enry Raccoon was mixing pots of paint. He was mixing a rainbow of color.

Edgar cheered up. Henry was always good for a laugh.

"Painting?" asked Edgar.

"Sort of," said Henry.

Henry was mixing red and yellow together in one pot. The orange looked like a summer sunset.

"A year goes by so fast," said Edgar. "Birthdays come and birthdays go. Birthdays roll around so fast it makes your head spin."

"Who says your head is spinning?" asked Henry.

"I'm talking about birthdays," said Edgar. "Summer birthdays. What if you had a summer birthday?" Edgar wanted to give Henry just a *tiny* clue. "Let's say your birthday was this week," continued Edgar. "This very week. Let's say your birthday was this very day. Then it would be your birthday this very minute. Isn't it a wonder?"

But Henry wasn't listening to Edgar.
He was laying out a big sheet of paper
and getting ready to paint. He wasn't
good for a laugh today.

Edgar sighed and slowly walked
away.

"I don't get it," he said. "Last year
everyone remembered. Last year
I had a wonderful balloon day.
This year . . . nothing."

Edgar stopped in his tracks. "Maybe I've got the wrong day!" he shouted. "Maybe today isn't my birthday after all!"

Edgar ran as fast as a badger
can run.

Surprise!

*E*dgar ran up the path to his house. He ran inside and right to the calendar in the kitchen. There was a big red circle around TODAY.

"My birthday *is* today," sighed Edgar. "My birthday is today and no one knows it."

Edgar sighed again and slumped into a chair. He stared out the window. He forgot about lunch. He forgot about his afternoon nap. He just sat and stared out the window.

"My birthday is going," he said. "My birthday is going fast. Soon my birthday will be gone. And I haven't even *one* balloon to show for it."

Suddenly there was a loud knock.
Edgar plodded to the door and
opened it.

"SURPRISE!" shouted all his friends.

Henry and Sally held up a sign.

Duncan handed Edgar a cake. It
was Edgar's favorite, banana-grub.

And there were balloons—bunches and bunches of balloons.

There were orange, purple, and green balloons. There were yellow, red, and blue balloons.

There was even a balloon tied to a basket! It was purple and gold and filled with hot air. It was the biggest balloon Edgar had ever seen.

"Hop on board, Edgar," said Sally.

"Time for the ride of your life," said Duncan.

"Up, up, and away!" cried Amanda.

Edgar was floating. Edgar was light. Edgar Badger was the happiest badger in the forest.